Fred Rogers PRODUCTIONS

Donkey Hodie™

Donkey Hodie Helps an Elephant

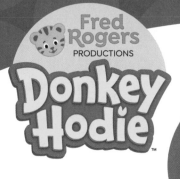

adapted by **Tina Gallo**
based on the screenplay **"A Big Favor For Grampy"**
written by **Adam Rudman and David Rudman**

Ready-to-Read

Simon Spotlight
New York London Toronto Sydney New Delhi

SIMON SPOTLIGHT
An imprint of Simon & Schuster Children's Publishing Division
1230 Avenue of the Americas, New York, New York 10020
This Simon Spotlight edition December 2021

Donkey Hodie is produced by Fred Rogers Productions and Spiffy Pictures.

Manufactured in the United States of America 1021 LAK
10 9 8 7 6 5 4 3 2 1
ISBN 978-1-5344-9941-6 (hc)
ISBN 978-1-5344-9940-9 (pbk)
ISBN 978-1-5344-9942-3 (ebook)

“Hi, Donkey Hodie,”
Grampy Hodie said.
“Will you please walk
my pet elephant, Gregory?”

Donkey was excited.

“I, Donkey Hodie, will take Gregory for a walk!” she said.

"Are you ready, Gregory?"

Donkey asked.

Gregory did not move.

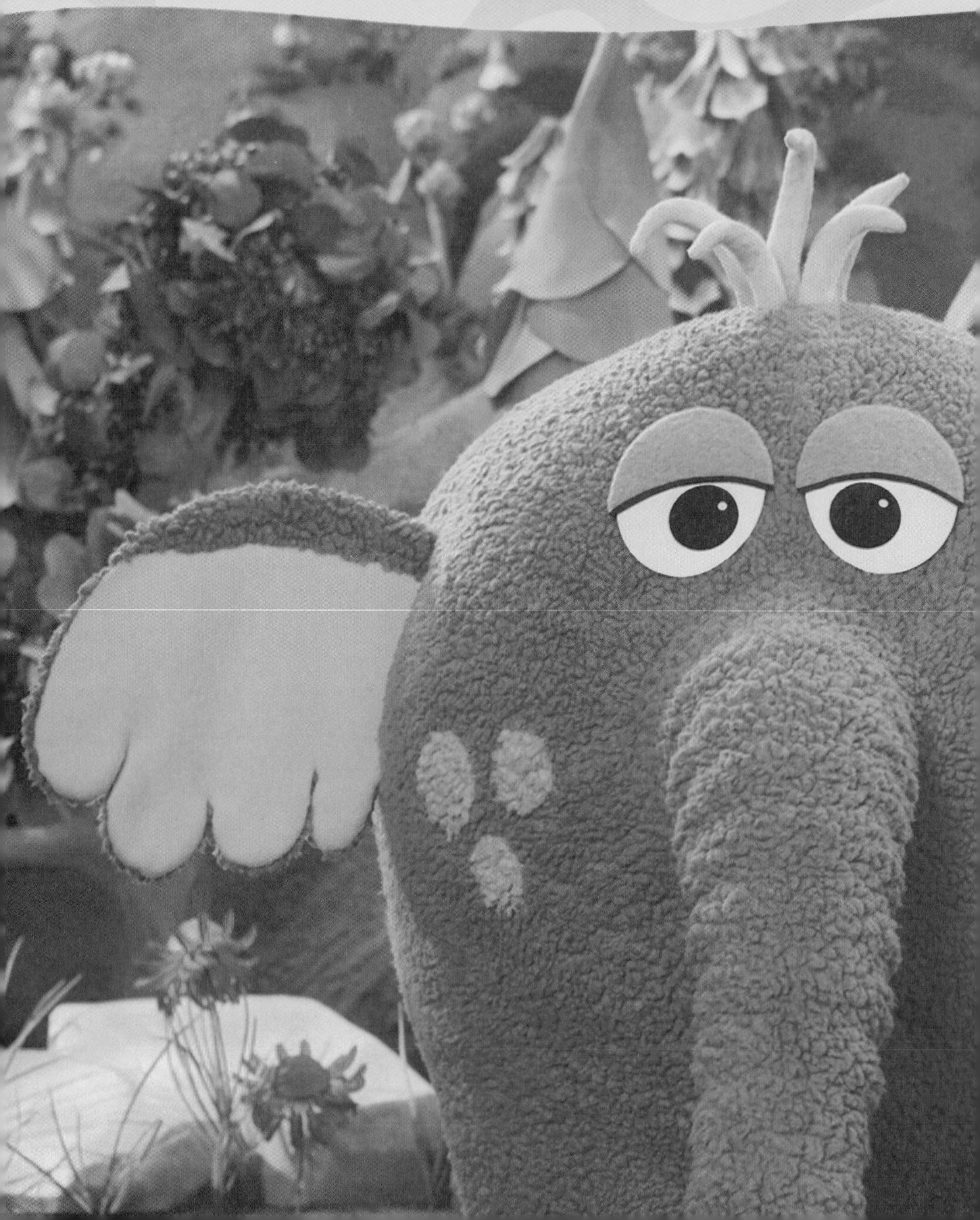

"Think, Donkey Hodie, think!" Donkey said.

Just then, Purple Panda stopped by on his skateboard.

"Gregory will not move,"
Donkey told Panda.

Donkey looked at
the skateboard.
She had an idea!

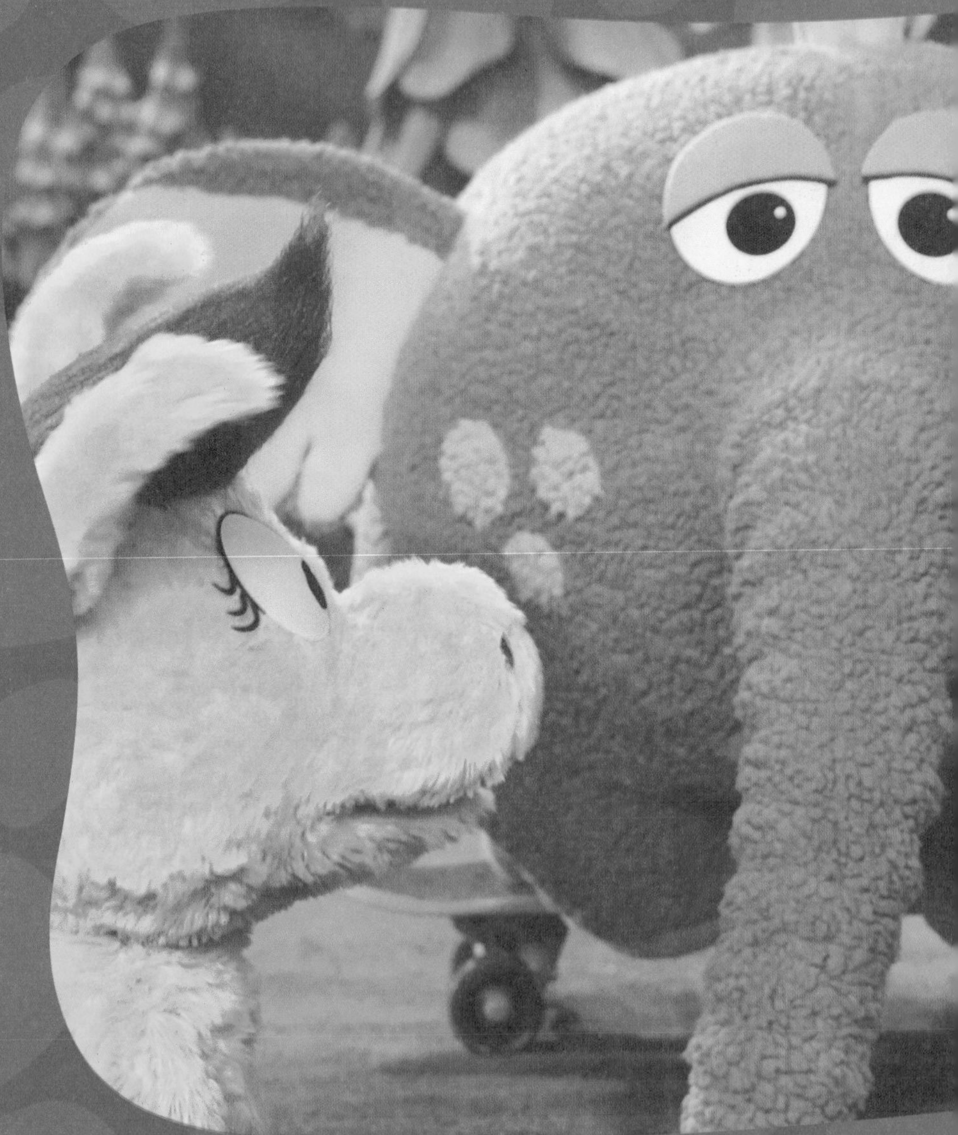

She and Panda put Gregory on the skateboard.

The skateboard rolled away with Gregory on it!

Donkey and Panda stopped the skateboard, and Gregory got off it.

"Sorry I could not help,
but I have to go now,"
Panda said.

"Can I help?"

Duck Duck asked.

"My book says elephants like to eat peanuts. . . ."

Donkey put a huge peanut on a fishing pole.
Gregory did not move.

Then Bob Dog said
Gregory might want
to fetch a ball.

Bob Dog threw the ball.
Gregory did not move.

The ball landed in a nest.
Donkey went to get it
and frowned.

Clyde the Cloud said,

"You look upset, Donkey."

"Gregory will not move,"

she said.

"When I feel upset,
I sing a little song,"
Clyde said.

“I just say, ‘Stop! Stop!’
Take a breath,
breathe in deep down
to my tummy. . . .”

Then he sang,
"When I take a deep breath,
I blow my troubles away!"

Donkey took a deep breath.

She felt calm and ready to solve her problem.

Back in the yard, Donkey saw a radio with toys that belonged to Gregory. She had a new idea.

She turned on the radio,

and music played.

Gregory moved!

Gregory loved walking

with music!

Donkey was so proud that she walked Gregory and helped Grampy!